DUCK and COVER

Jackie Urbanovic

HarperCollinsPublishers

Thanks to Maria, for her
encouragement and laughter.
Thanks also for all the critters
who bless our journey.

Duck and Cover
Copyright © 2009 by Jackie Urbanovic

Printed in the U.S.A.

Library of Congress Cataloging-in-Publication Data is available.
ISBN 978-0-06-121444-8 (trade bdg.)
ISBN 978-0-06-121445-5 (lib. bdg.)

Typography by Rachel Zegar
1 2 3 4 5 6 7 8 9 10
❖
First Edition

EVERYONE WELCOME

KNOCK, KNOCK, KNOCK!
HELP!
KNOCK, KNOCK, KNOCK!
HELP!

"**W**ho could that be?"
asked Irene.

ANOTHER
DUCK?

"HELP!
If the zoo detective finds
me, I'm a goner!"

"Why are they after you?" asked Irene.

"I just had a snack! Okay, so it was someone's pet. I didn't know that!" he said.

"PLEASE DON'T EAT US!" everyone screamed.

Max was afraid too, but he
remembered what it was like to be
in trouble and alone. Now it was
his turn to help someone else.

"Uh, hello. I'm Max," he said, shaking.

"Hello, Max. I'm Harold," said the alligator.

"My mouth is big and my appetite is bigger, but I'm not dangerous. REALLY. Please hide me!" Harold pleaded.

PLEASE,
IRENE?

"I believe him, Irene.
Can we rescue Harold
like you rescued me?"
asked Max.

Reluctantly Irene opened the door all the way. "Come on out, wherever you are!" Max called.

WHERE'D EVERYONE GO?

FAR TOO MANY TEETH.

"It's safe, and Harold really needs our help. Now everyone THINK. Where can we hide an alligator in this house?"

NICE SHADE OF GREEN.

AWFULLY BIG.

"How about the bread box?" said Tawny.

THUNK! OW!
THUNK!

"Nope, too small," said Irene.

"We could disguise him as a lamp!" suggested Chloe.

"I don't think so!" said Brody. "We need a brighter idea."

"I know! The basement!" said Scrappy.

NO NO NO NO
NO NO NO
NO NO
NO!

"IT'S DARK, AND
THERE ARE SPIDERS!"
screamed Harold.

"Any other ideas?"
asked Max.

"Ma'am, have you or your duck seen this alligator?" asked the detective.

"Why, no sir. No gators here," said Irene nervously.

"Dogs and cats and birds and rabbits . . . but no alligators," said Max.

"Well, give me a call if you see anything," he said. "And keep your eyes peeled. He's full of teeth, and dangerous."

"What a close call!" said Irene, closing the door.

"I could use something to drink," said Max.

"How about everyone else?"

"Lovely," said Harold.

"What do you take with your tea,
Harold?" asked Max.

"Scones, cakes, itty-bitty sandwiches—," he began.
"I MEAN, milk or sugar?" Max interrupted.
"Both, please. A little bit of everything is always
tasty," said Harold.

After tea and a lot of talking, they still weren't sure how to keep Harold—or themselves—safe. So they decided to sleep on it. In Irene's room. With the door locked tight.

The next morning Max made his usual breakfast of pancakes with a special tuna sauce for the cats. Everyone was finished eating except for Harold.

"Got anything else to nibble on?" he asked, looking around.

Remembering that they would be safe as long as Harold was full, the cats ran to the cupboard.

"Salmon, yes!" said Max. "Should we broil it with lemon or—"

"JUST GIVE HIM A CAN OPENER!" said Dakota.

"Delish!" exclaimed Harold.

Later that day Max came up with a brilliant idea. Now they knew exactly what they'd do if the detective returned.

Until then, all they had to do was
to keep Harold hidden. And fed.

NEED A SNACK, HAROLD?

They didn't have to wait long.

OPEN UP!
WE KNOW HE'S
IN THERE!

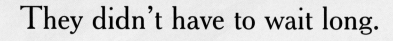

"Ma'am, your neighbors called the zoo. They reported seeing someone suspiciously green in your backyard," he said.

"Okay, Harold. It's no use hiding. Come on out," said Irene.

"WHAT?!" yelled the detective. "WHO'S the REAL Harold?"

"I really need to talk to him," he said. "LOOK!"
"Gator Goof. Zoo wishes to right wrong," Irene read.

"The dog we thought Harold ate wasn't the girl's PET DOG. It was her HOT DOG. We misunderstood. So Harold, whichever one is you, would you please come home?" he pleaded.

"Of course I'd like to come home, but I hate to leave my new family," said Harold. "I love you all so much, I could eat you up."

But to the cats' relief, he just hugged them close.